7.95

E   Reed, Tom
c.3   Melissa on parade

MELISSA ON PARADE

BRADBURY PRESS   SCARSDALE, NEW YORK

MELISSA ON PARADE

WRITTEN AND ILLUSTRATED
BY
TOM REED

The text of this book is set in Helvetica Light. The illustrations are pen and water-color drawings, reproduced in full color.

Library of Congress Cataloging in Publication Data
Reed, Tom. Melissa on parade.
Summary: While everyone else is watching the parade, Melissa spots a fleeing bank robber.
[1. Parades -- Fiction. 2. Robbers and outlaws – Fiction]
I. Title.
PZ7.R2534Me   [E]   78-26339
ISBN 0-87888-143-3

To Mom and Dad
and Ken

Melissa was a little girl who loved a good parade.
She and Ralph and Winston, who were her faithful dogs,
would try to help each marching band that came into the town.

One day at the parade grounds, Melissa saw her chance.

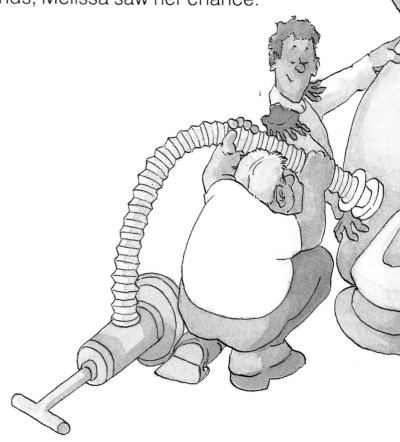

Eagerly, the young girl asked to pump parade balloons.
Bandmaster Riley simply smiled, and called her arms "pint-sized."

Then she tried to play a tune, but *everything* went wrong.

And when she tried to march instead, the bandmaster just groaned.
He stared at her, and then he said, "Who put such ideas in your head?"

And for Melissa, that was how things *always* seemed to go...

Soon the parade got under way,
and what a sight it was.
Everyone kept beat and step,
and music filled the air.
But Melissa, sad Melissa,
did not even care.
"Watching things, you call *that* fun?"
she sighed, and turned away.

But hardly had she said these words
when something caught her eye:
a robber fleeing from a bank ran to the crowd to hide...

...and Melissa watched.

Yes, Melissa watched.

And when a mother looked away, that clever robber struck.
He snatched a baby up and out, then climbed into his place.

And that poor mother rolled the robber,
not her baby, home.

"That mother needs help!"
Melissa shouted loudly, but no one seemed to listen.

"Well, then it's up to us," she said to Baby, who agreed.

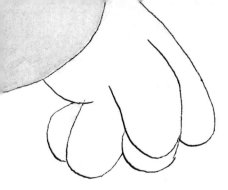

Melissa, Ralph, and Winston, and even Baby too,
jumped right into the avenue, in front of everyone.

Then they began to march and dance...

and swing and jiggle too.

They tried their hand at *anything* to make the people watch.

The balloonmen loved Melissa's act,
and clapped to show they did.
But since they could not clap *and* hold,
that soon meant trouble overhead.

Melissa told the bandmaster all that she had seen.
"It is just your help we need. That is all," she said.

As Riley paused to think this through,
he glanced above and groaned.
"Oh, no!" he cried.
"Big Henry's loose. He must not get away!"

Big Henry, the parade balloon, was the biggest of them all.
Eight solid men with sixteen arms could hardly hold him down.

Big Henry floated up and up, and no one could get near him.
But then he lodged between the roofs in a very useful spot.

For Henry was a cop balloon, and from his vantage point,
he gazed right through the window at none other than the crook!

The crook let out a cry because his nightmares had come true.

And before too long, Riley arrived, and got things in control.

Melissa received a handsome medal from the mayor himself.

And even Baby got to be an official balloon-holder,
a thing which tickled everyone…

...a bit *too* much for Baby's taste...

Since Baby, after all,
preferred spots closer to the ground!